ALEXANDRA KIRSCHBAUM | MARCELLUS M. MENKE

DELETED

AF189096

Alexandra Kirschbaum | Marcellus M. Menke

DELETED

WHAT HAPPENS WHEN WE FORGET HOW TO THINK

GRAPHIC NOVEL.

Edition HIC<
|BLACK HOLE PUBLISHING|*

Alexandra Kirschbaum | Marcellus M. Menke
Deleted
What happens when we forget how to think
Graphic Novel

Edition HIC< |BLACK H⊙LE PUBLISHING|*

Text: Alexandra Kirschbaum
Illustrations and captions: Marcellus M. Menke

„Deleted" is the revised and augmented version of the novella
„Graphene Neurons" (ISBN 9783756895601)

Layout, cover design and typesetting: Marcellus M. Menke
marcellus.m.menke@m4art.de

Bibliographic information of the German National Library:
The German National Library lists this publication in the
Deutsche Nationalbibliografie; Detailed bibliographic data are
available on the Internet via dnb.dnb.de.

© 2023 Marcellus M. Menke

Production and publishing: BoD – Books on Demand,
Norderstedt

ISBN: 9783751953825

Idea

Tó wondered why, in the default
setting, in nearly all systems, it
was always a woman's face that
visualized the counterpart.

Conversation

The conversation with the digital assistant had been very unpleasant. A few times Tó had even reached out for the normally hardly used keyboard, and that not because of a special character that was not properly resolved by the speech recognition.

He had already realized that it would not be so easy to explain the project to the system, but, before he could submit a grant application, he needed a calculation, and if everything had gone well, he would have gotten a reliable prognosis right away — that's what the system was for, after all. But it had not gone well.

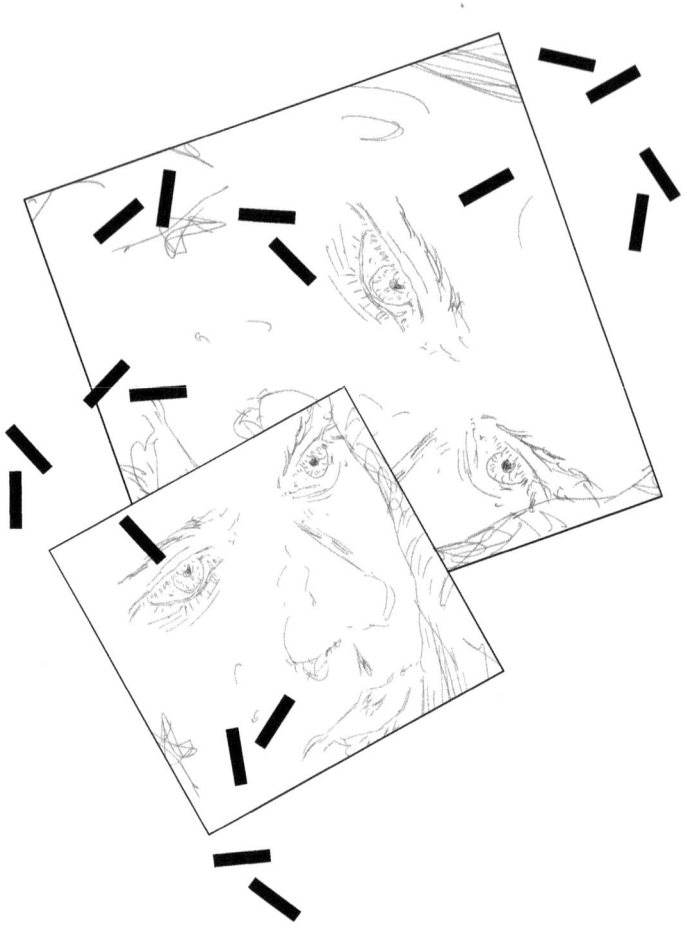

Leap innovation. That wasn't just the next logical step. It was a whole lot of steps at once. Of course, there was also the possibility of failure. But perhaps he shouldn't have said that.

The system simply did not understand that one could also calculate with pencil and paper. Of course, AlRith and all the tools they had developed here at the institute could be used to write highly efficient functional algorithms. But sometimes you could just have a good idea without a computers help. Of course, new hardware models could also be computed on the highly potent classical machines. In the beginning, quantum computers were also simulated on existing machines. But there were leap innovations. Something really new could also be fundamentally different. The fact that it could not be simulated on the current supercomputers did not automatically mean that it could not work.

Probably what he had in mind was somehow like an attempt to convince a system that thought it had found a solution for everything — and from a certain point of view the system did have a solution for everything — that there were also solutions outside its imaginary space.

Was that possible?

Efri was one of the few here who could really listen. What she said was never trivial.

Offer

"You just have to accept that," Efrie said, "no one is going to give you half a million simply because you think you have a good idea."

Tó looked into his coffee. She was right. Of course she was right.

"Well, I can help you out a little," Efrie said, "got some spare capacity, I can give it to you."

Tó smiled. That was an offer. Efrie was the best on the team. Two or three days from her was more than a start-up funding from the grant fund.

A new project, that was always like diving into a
sparkling whirlpool. There was so much liveliness
and joy. That made him euphoric every time.

Handwork

Actually, he only had the three sheets with the hand-written sketches. There was already a problem when scanning them. The OCR software resolved the formula characters completely differently. Obviously, the system did not know his notation style. The assignment of the operators was completely unusable. Doing it by hand would take time. In addition, he noticed that some formulas could not be represented in the software in this way. He would have to develop models there himself. He might even have to write a whole new rule set of logic frames.

Julia was sure that Efri was in love with Tó. But
that was nonsense, of course. „If at all, maybe in
his avatar," Efri told the friend, when she didn't
let up and again and again started with it. But
her some how sharp smile seemed a bit forced and
couldn't really cover up the rising embarrassment.

Engagement

Efri was still sitting in front of her computer. That was quite a complex task she had gotten herself into. But it also was a really interesting idea, the most interesting she had come across in the last two years. She couldn't understand why her colleagues were so skeptical.

Of course, she shouldn't have spend so much time in creating Tó's avatar. For the internal projects, most of the colleagues here had only very simple representatives. You could see the basic facial characteristics, the hair color, of course, and the shape of the head. If you met the colleague in person in the hallway, you knew who he or she was. But only very few colleagues had photorealistic avatars. But that was possible. The data was available. Efri found that it was easier to work on a project if the details of the visual user interface were right. She needed that. In all projects she took care, that her avatar always was photorealistic and in high-resolution.

Not everyone on the team understood Efri's commitment to Tó's project. Alain had once asked her about her time management. That was almost something like an open confrontation. At least that's how Efri had perceived it. And formally, he was right, of course. There wasn't even an application for the project.

16

Amazing

The first results from the colleagues of the materials testing department had arrived. Efri had asked Daniel to make a small sample and measure it. Tó was right. His graphene constructions actually behaved as he had predicted and that at room temperature and normal pressure.

That was amazing, actually already a small sensation, if that should prove to be true. Of course, the whole thing was not yet something that could be written into an application. The way Tó handled the mathematics was somewhat unconventional, and if they were unlucky, the values from the lab that seem to fit so well could just be a simple measurement error. She would have preferred a good theoretical foundation. But if Tó was right, then this could be a really big thing. Efri was really thrilled.

Just as a test, Efri had used the voice of Tó's avatar to read a children's book. The quality was astonishing. It was more than HD audio. Even sentence and speech melody were reproduced almost perfectly. Efris six-year-old son was thrilled.

Data

The project was getting a bit big. Efri wasn't sure about the backup routines. After all, there was no project number yet, and to the system, her ideas and calculations were simply incoherent notes.

To be on the safe side, Efri made copies on an external data carrier. She had the opportunity to do that, which was a privilege. She used it abundantly, even for other projects. In her office, data media marked with small labels were piled up. Most were offline and only connected to the system for the time of data transfer. Cold Storage. An old-fashioned concept, but it protected against the system's unpredictable erasure routines.

Efri's relationship with her colleagues in the technical department was very good. But she hadn't thought that they would get so deeply involved right away. After all, what she and Tó were doing was actually only a preliminary study. There was neither a budget nor an official order.

Gamma

The micromanipulators used to create the prototypes of the graphene structures Tó constructed could also be used as a measuring instrument. A kind of sub-quantum scanning force field microscope. The fact that each individual atom could be positioned individually had long been state of the art. But that one could now see an individuality in each atom, that was new. Nor had this been envisaged in the classical models before.

"It's like looking from above at a large crowd of people, for example, people walking into a subway station," Tó said in his smoothest avatar-explanatory-voice, giving a very real smile to Efri's astonished face, "from above, they're just little dots moving around, and you can statistically predict their movement. But when you get closer, you see that people are individual. Every face is different. And just in that way also each atom is individual. Of course, it has no consciousness. It's not a living being, after all. But each atom is different. You can distinguish them individually, not just group them by their isotopes."

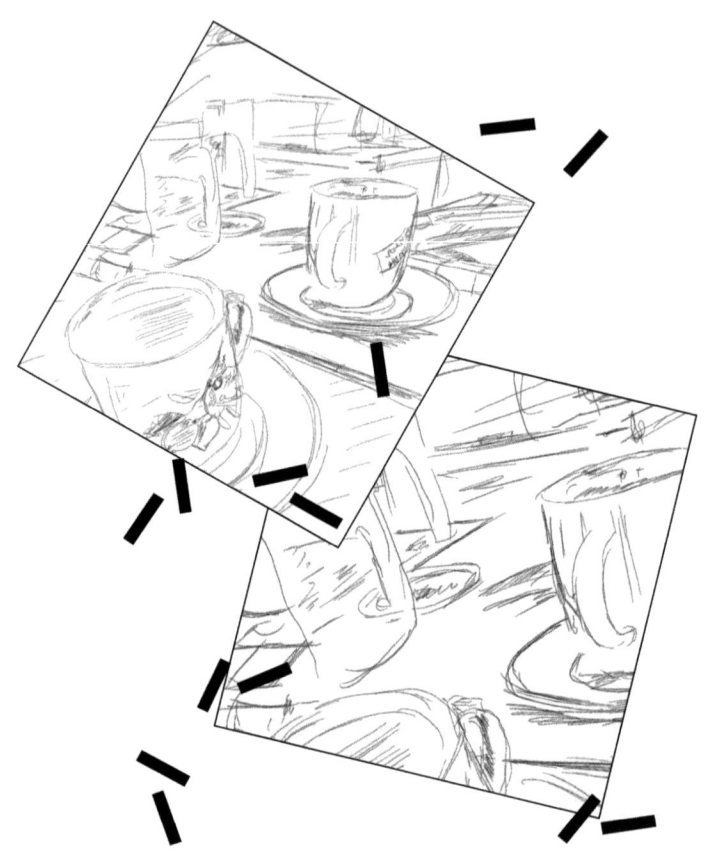

Sometimes just a cup of tea was enough for him. It didn't always had to be a full breakfast.

Breakfast

Tó watched the machine prepareing the breakfast.

Seeing the precision with which the machine poured the whisked scrambled eggs onto the surface of the pan always made him want to do it himself. He let it be. He had tried it once. It had gone wrong, thoroughly. From his father he still had, way in the back of the kitchen cabinet, a skillet. The hardware was there. He could have done it himself.

To impress Rachel, the first woman he had made love to, he had once tried to make a naturalist breakfast. But you just couldn't do it as perfect as the machines. You couldn't.

As a child, his father had refused to use the machines for quite some time. This was diagnosed as a behavioral disorder and there was something politically disreputable about it. The Naturalists also existed as a subversive political movement. They didn't like machines, which was nonsense. That wouldn't work, a life without machines.

No one in his right mind would want to wash his clothes by hand. Lisa had done that with her blouses. She also thought for a while that she had to iron them

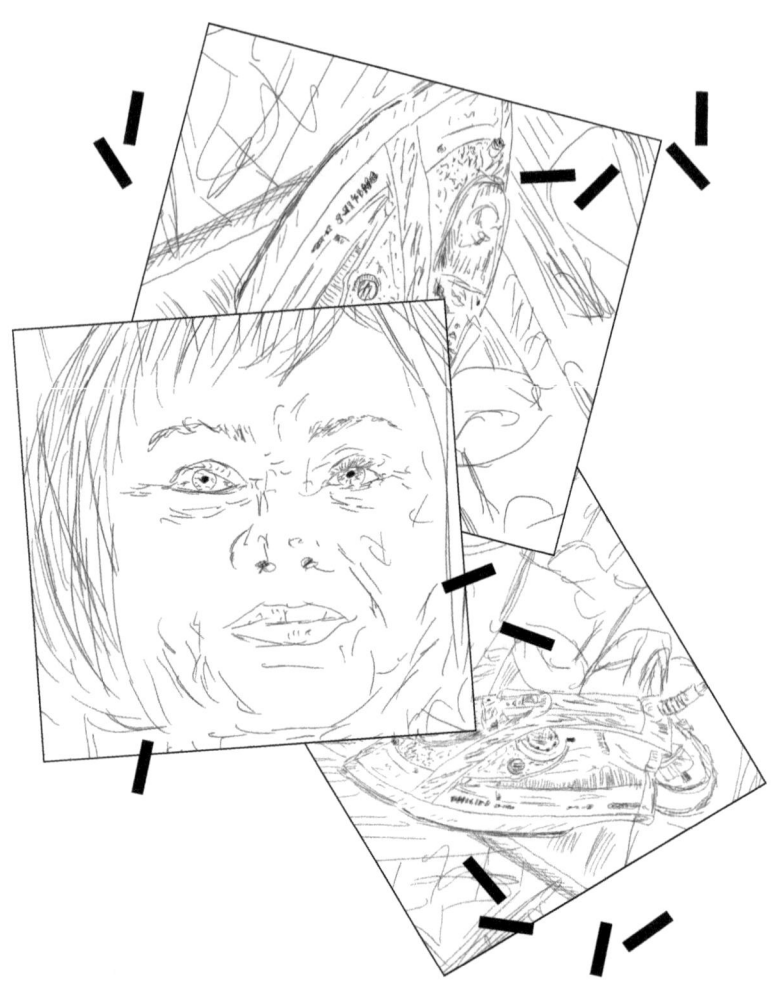

As a historical object, Tó considered Lisa's iron interesting. But he would never have thought of pouring water into it through one of the holes and then connecting it to the household power grid with a cable.

by hand. The outcome had been horrible. The iron she used was, of course, not networked, not even approved anymore. It was a model from her great-grandmother. She could have set the whole apartment on fire with it.

You of course had to turn off the smoke detector, because the steam from the iron would immediately have set off the alarm. The room sensor system was not set up for such old-fashioned devices. There even wasn't a simple subroutine running without connection to network and sensors.

He had separated from Lisa after half a year. You couldn't live with someone like that in the long run. Somehow one had to know in which time one lived. One should accept the realities, idealism or not.

Fairy tales: Why didn't he dream of Hans Christian Andersen's Little Mermaid, if at all it had to be a story from his childhood?

26

Dream

Sun was over the sea. Water on the right, water on the left, water in front of him, water behind him. The small boat was moving fast, the water foamed at the bow. But he could not make out any direction. Probably the boat was always going straight ahead. The water was an infinitely straight surface, no edges discernible, it seemed. The sun was much too far away to see its change in size, which had to be there, had to be observable. The boat was moving, but he did not have the impression that they were getting closer to a destination.

It appeared quite unexpectedly, a small tube, a periscope. Then the back of an emerging submarine. A powerful vessel. The eddies threatened to pull the small motorboat down. Tó's grip on the railing tightened. But that wouldn't have helped him if he capsized.

"Nemo," it went through his head. It was crazy what he was getting himself into here. As a simulation, it would have been an adventure. But this wasn't a simulation. Sure it was real.

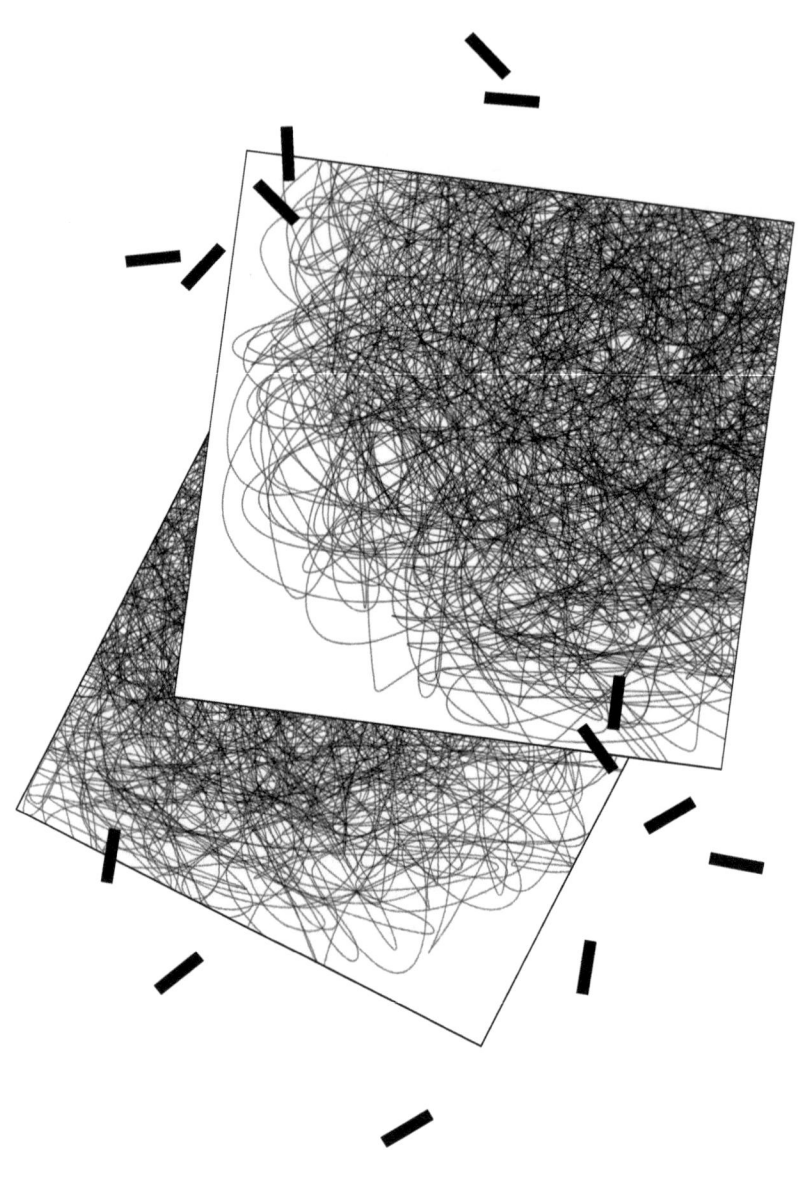

New

He woke up.

That was terrible. He wanted to do something new, something really new, and instead he got lost in the future stories of the past.

Today's machines did their brainwork in the same way as their inventors did it, but they were dead, several hundred years already. Progress only was to be found in the infinite expanse of thinking networks of self-organizing neurons, and graphene was the material from which these neurons could be built. The material of the future. He was sure.

Yes, he needed a planet, he would place the graphene neurons there. Neurons made of high-purity carbon, self-organizing. They would turn the whole planet into a single thinking machine. Maybe he should use a gaseous planet. In principle, however, it didn't matter what elements the planet was made of or what state of matter they were in. The neurons dissolved all matter to a plasma. From the plasma they built, in

In the chats for some time it was fashionable
that men wore glasses. Some kind of superfluous
retro trend. Tó thought glasses were terrible.

order to replicate themselves, the graphene of which they consisted. Only big was the planet to be. As much mass as possible.

If I would tell this in a circle of colleagues, I would land immediately in the loony bin, he thought and crumpled up the piece of paper on which he had written the functions, to let it disappear in his trouser pocket.

The chat bot noticed his hasty movement and scanned him. But it didn't get to him. Obviously, he did not or could not recognize what revolutionary idea was there on the piece of paper. Writing on paper, with a pen, that was only tolerated. That was no longer supported. Who was still doing that? On the tablets and pads, people used pens, but they were intelligent, not like a pencil, which only created a trace of the path of the hand that guided it.

It would never happen. Never, he thought, and never was zero, the first zero, the beginning of time. And then it would be pure thinking, clear simple thoughts and everything would run according to the laws of reason.

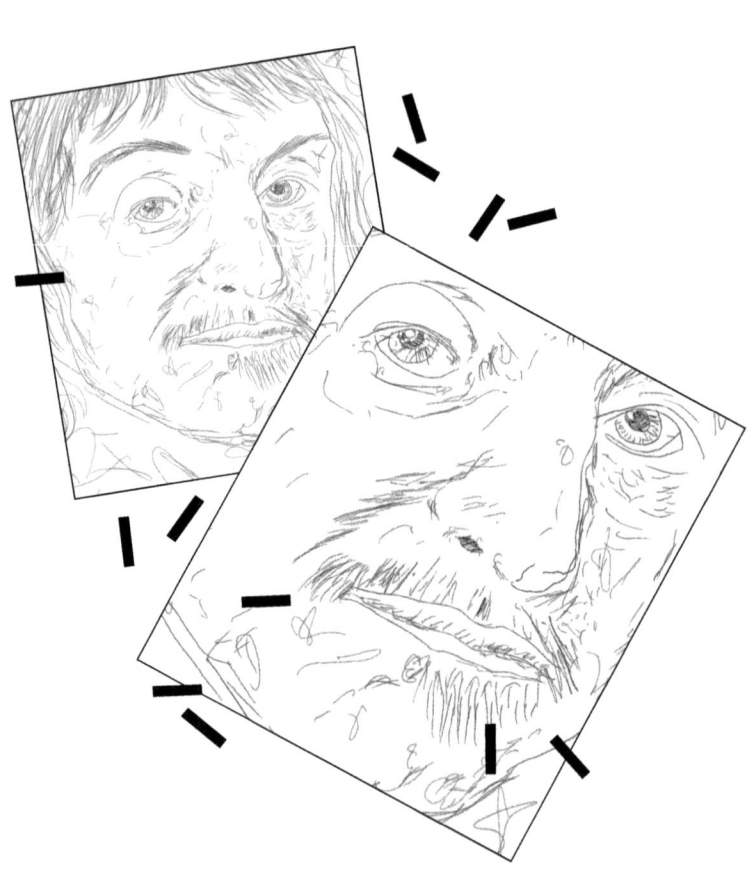

Sometimes Tó wished he could travel through time. What would René Descartes, for example, have said about his thoughts? That would be an interesting question.

Copies

The result of the check was devastating. With the automatic in-depth check the algorithm found 260 plagiarisms in the thirty pages of the paper. A good 60 percent of the sentences and 47 percent of the parts of the sentences were found verbatim in other sources. In terms of content, 80 percent of the thoughts were already in other papers. He looked at the details of the list: 12 times Jules Verne, 42 times Star Trek, 11 times Perry Rhodan, three times Robbi Tobbi und das Fliewatüüt. Fliewatüüt? Tó paused. The whole list seemed strange to him. He hadn't submitted a paper on the history of media, culture or literature. It was a technical scientific thesis paper. Yes, he had written text, because for what he wanted to do in the research project there was no mathematical formulation and no established terminology yet. Yes, he had also written something about inventiveness. But Fliewatüüt?

He ran a web search. First hit: Boy Lornsen: Robbi, Tobbi und das Fliewatüüt, German children's book, 256

Perhaps at some point the system would find out
that he had copied from the German 1986 Duden.
All the words he had used in the application were
listed there in alphabetical order. Of course, he had
not used all the words and had also changed the
order. — Tó thought that one should not make flat
jokes, they were caught up too fast by reality.

pages, publisher: Thienemann Verlag; edition: 32nd (August 1, 1967). ISBN 978-3522111805.

Tó shook his head. Surely this couldn't be true. Yes, he had submitted the text in German. That was his mother tongue. There were now very good translation programs for the commission; they were certified and translated better than a human translator. It shouldn't matter whether he wrote his application in English or German. It couldn't be that the database for German was now already so small that they had to resort to a children's book. He clicked on the entry to see the details. The first connector was "Tó." That was his name. And where did it appear in the children's book? When he opened the details menu he couldn't believe it: "]Tó[in this contents seen as short form of]Tobbi[obviously childhood fantasies; parallels 93.78%".

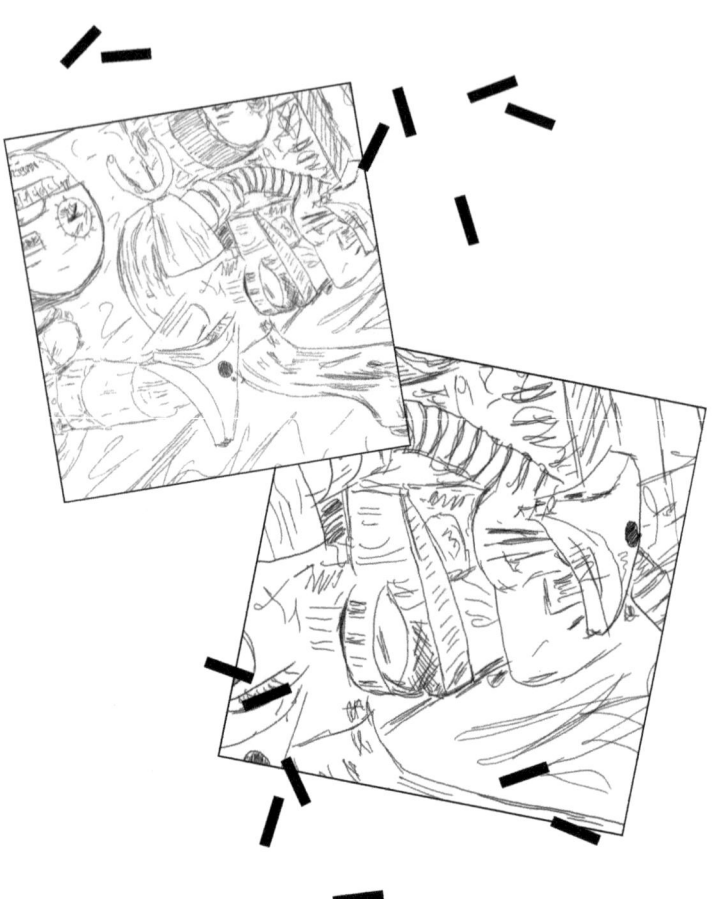

The protection of historical monuments could sometimes produce strange blossoms. In the bathroom, for example, the faucets had to be copied from the design of the 1970s because the bathroom had been installed in 1975. The house was from 1880 and even in 1975, the installation of the bathroom was a violation of the regulations for the protection of historical monuments that were in effect at the time. Today, the violation of that time was worth protecting. Tó did not understand that. But he liked the old faucets.

Bath

Tó was tired. He went into the bathroom to refresh himself with a shower. He would just forget the whole thing, would continue to do his work at the institute and stop applying for special projects. There was no need to do that. In fact, it was probably much better for one's career to do one's work quite uneventful. Of course the rejection of the application would be negative for his evaluation. But he would work off that. There were so many routine tasks, to be processed quite inconspicuously and without any risk. The results were usually practically a foregone conclusion. A lapse like that, it wasn't a leg-breaker after all. Keep going. He just had to believe in himself.

He took a longer shower. It did him good to let the warm water run down his body. It was relaxing. He ignored the audible message that indicated he had exceeded the recommended shower time.

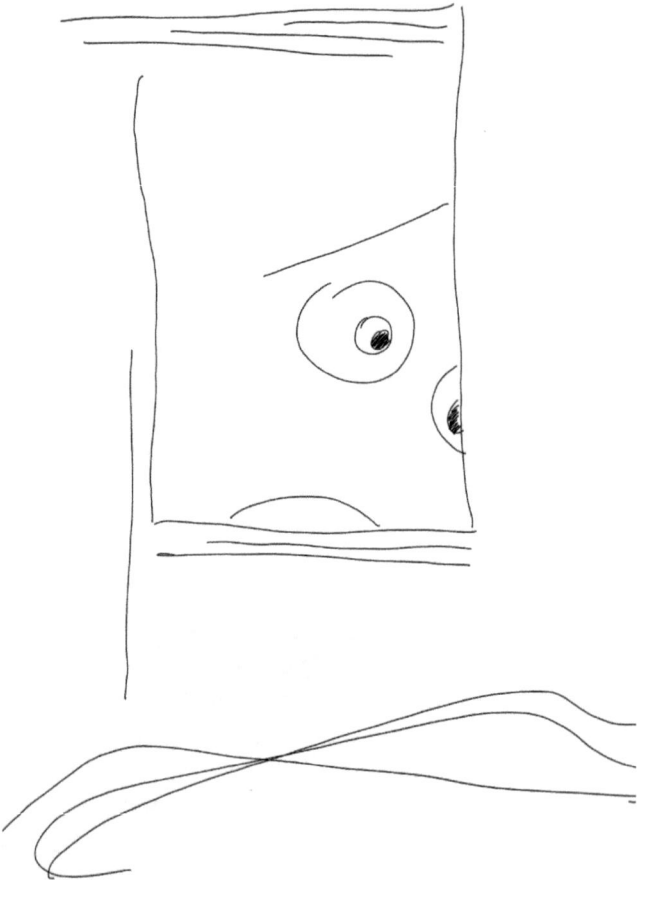

When he had had enough, he used a voice command to swing open the shower stall door, grabbed the towel and slowly dried himself off. He liked those big fuzzy soft bath towels.

With the bath towel tied around his hips, he headed for the hallway. But the door of the bathroom did not open. There was still too much humidity in the bathroom. The automatic door lock was a safety mechanism of the house electronics. It was necessary so that the installation of a bathroom could be approved in this old building. The rooms were listed as historical monuments. In the salon, yes there was a real salon here, there were paintings by old masters, they didn't belong to him of course but to the museum, but they were here in the heritage-listed apartment in their original environment. It was a privilege to be allowed to live in such an apartment. In return, one accepted that the home electronics were sometimes more powerful than the residents. He looked at the display: Three minutes to go. That was a long time. There was an air jam in duct four. Apparently, the tenant above him had also just taken a shower. The system was not designed to be used in the whole house at the same time, otherwise too many air ducts would have had to be built into the Wilhelminian-style house.

He had probably simply overheard the warning before taking the shower. Normally, when he entered the bathroom, there was always a notice if there might be a problem with the time of use.

He was still so lost in thought. Yes he was really done. Actually, he needed a vacation. No, nonsense, he

The days when the rejection letters were sent out were always horrible for Liv. So many hopes dashed in one fell swoop. But the system's decisions were rational and always well-founded. You couldn't make exceptions. Sometimes she was really depressed. She had often thought about changing jobs.

had just taken it, for this stupid project, in whose rejection explanation he had read something before the shower. He wouldn't read it all again. The tenor was clear, this was a complete rejection, scathing. The few details he had already looked into, so randomly, were enough for him. That was sufficient.

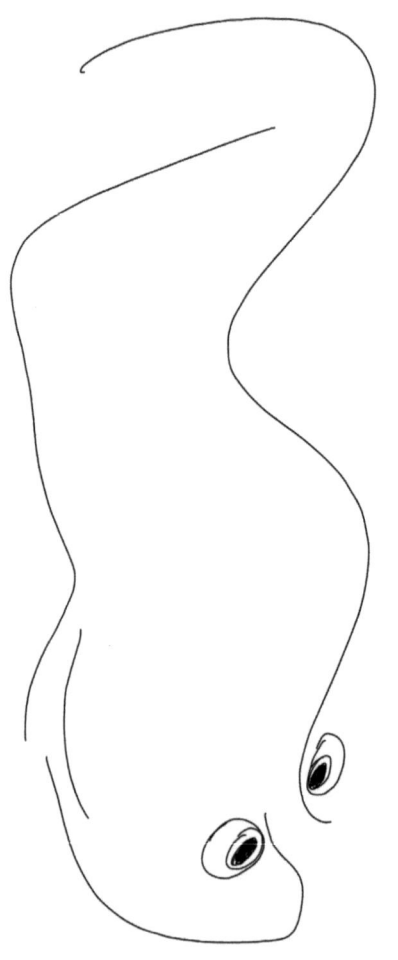

Tired

The bathroom door was still locked for 67 seconds, approximate value, it said on the display. He looked in the mirror. A tired face looked back at him through the steam. He touched the sensor area. The camera calculated the bathroom haze out of the image. Now he saw himself clearly. Wasn't any better. He should have turned on the beauty correction feature after all.

There was still some lint on the mirror. It was real, not in the computer image. He wiped it away with the towel.

A message appeared on the mirror: "This is the final copy of the displayed data. Do you really want to delete it?" Was the lint really real now, or just a faulty file projected into the mirror image?

"Delete it," he thought, "yeah right, delete it."

Who thought up such nonsense? A digital fluff on a mirror to make it look more natural. That was nonsense.

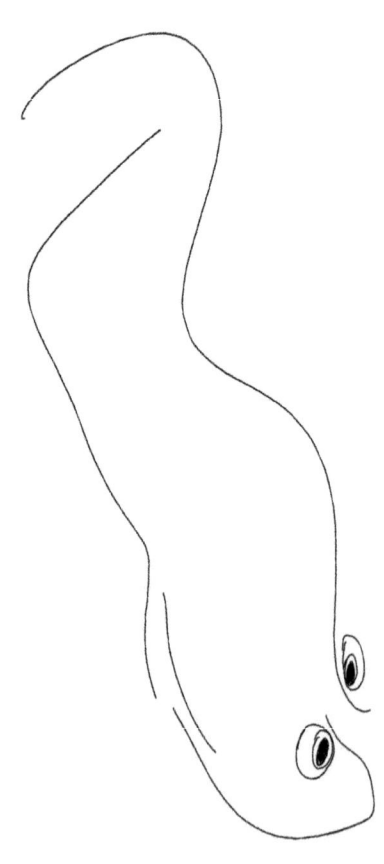

He would delete the application data right away too, just delete everything, the whole project. Deleting was a good solution. Then it would all be gone and tomorrow he would be back in the office, working on some boring paper of a supervisor, compiling measurements and data and contributing to the success of the institute. Childhood fantasies, my ass."

He wiped once more across the mirror.

"Double swipe gesture with soft real live object necessary to confirm this action."

Why were the system messages actually in English, he asked himself only now. Did the system no longer have the German language files? Was there a capacity problem?

The bathroom door was still closed. Okay, so the upstairs neighbor was probably taking a shower for a little longer. But no matter, he could also operate the system from here via the mirror. The towel was probably a "real live object" and "soft" too. It wouldn't scratch the mirror surface, even if he had to touch the sensor surface a little harder to confirm the action. The "double-swipe gesture" wasn't meant quite literally, but the impulse acting on the sensor matrix had to be a little firmer. Otherwise the commands with hyper-admin rights were not executed.

"Repeat this action to confirm. Warning: After your confirmation the last remaining copy will be deleted. Warning: You can't undo this action."

He didn't want to "undo" either quite the opposite, deleting it would undo the last three weeks and he'd start over as if all this stupid stuff hadn't happened, he

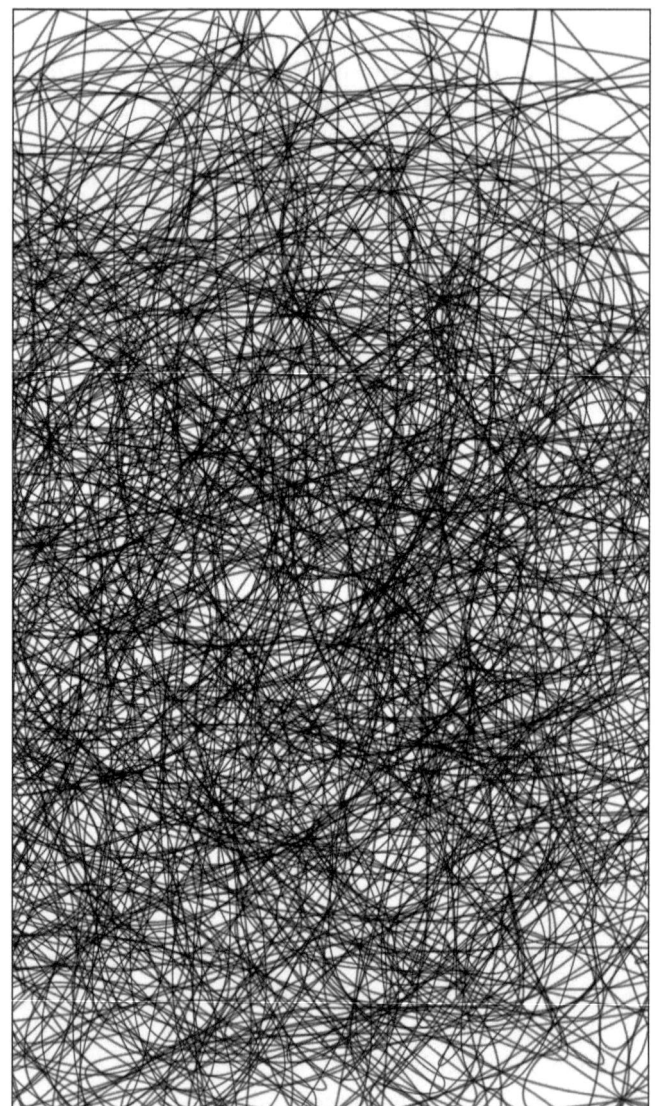

thought. He let the towel whiz twice with momentum onto the sensor surface.

The light went out. He disappeared. For a moment he thought he could still feel himself, but then he was no longer there.

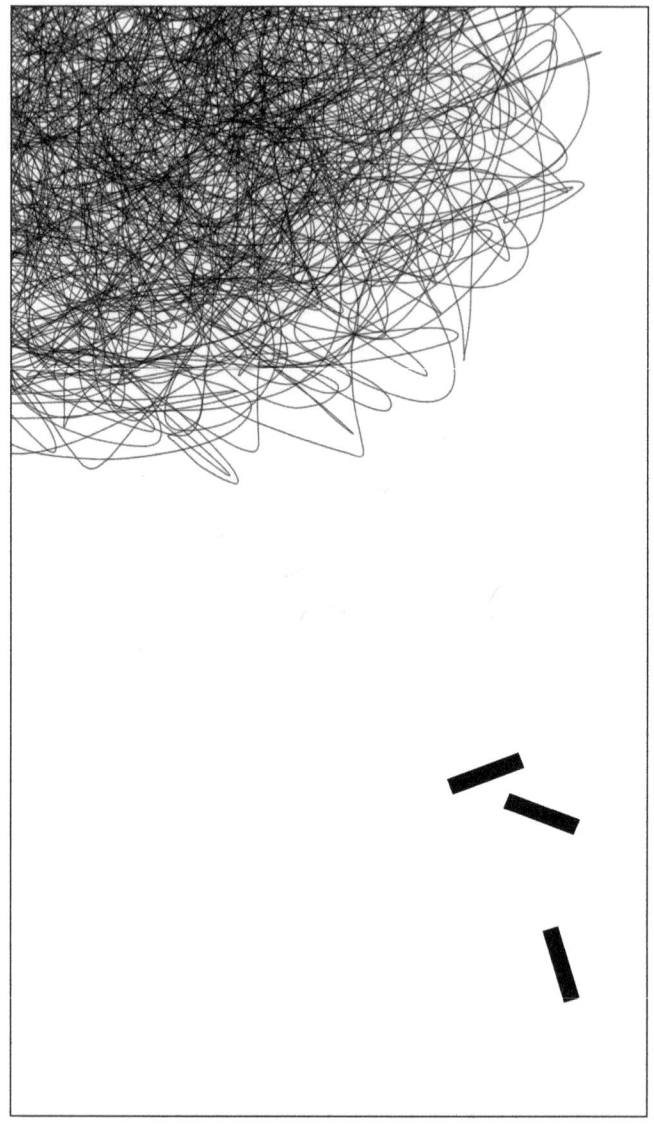

Vac

The home electronics released the bathroom door. The cleaning robot drove in. Analysis: Water, vaporous and in condensed drops [Caution: danger of slipping in area a12 to d17]. Carbon on the floor, range s6 to q12, powdery. Mass about 23.8 kg.

The robot passed the data to the head office of the home maintenance company. They requested a special machine for cleaning the bathroom. He would have had to change the damp room vacuum cleaner bags twelve times in order to vacuum all that up. That wasn't his job. That was supposed to be done by the bigger machine.

These humanoids' will to live was very underdeveloped, the robot thought as it drove out of the bathroom. They were amazingly unstable. A strangely high suicide rate. Yet they lived in the best apartments, and were looked after by a whole fleet of machines. A real pity about the fine carbon.

Aftermath

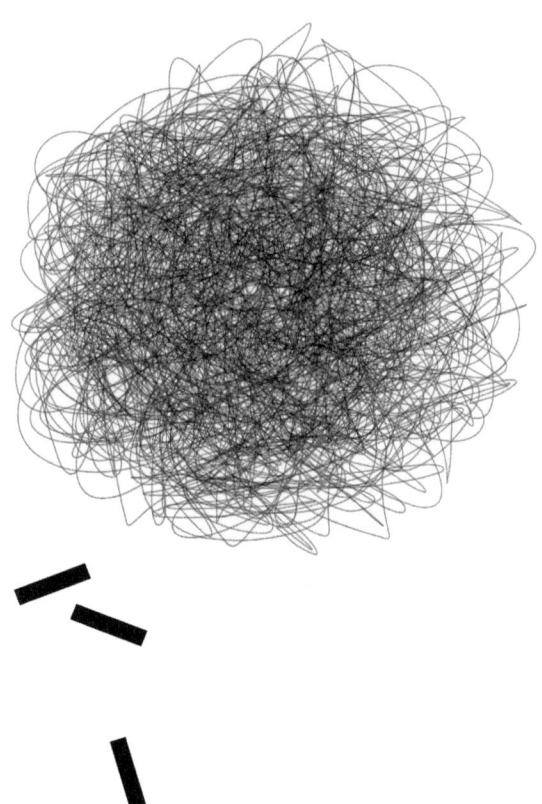

Displeased

The CEO of the home utility and maintenance company was displeased.

"Can't you get rid of them?"

"No," was the prompt response from the building management system, short and dry. "The gentlemen say they'll wait the prescribed five minutes. Otherwise, they'll override my code via the entrance area's NFC box and unlock access for themselves."

This must be something urgent. The CEO noticed his pulse going up. He was uncomfortable with strangers coming into his office. He hadn't received a visitor in years, so physical, real. Everything went via the systems. You only had to look at it once in a while, explain some of the not-so-familiar functions to a new customer in a phone call, before he then signed the premium contract. The brokers, yes, still had direct customer contact during the viewings. But everything else was digital.

Where was his jacket? It should have been cleaned long ago. It smelled. And somewhere he had a comb.

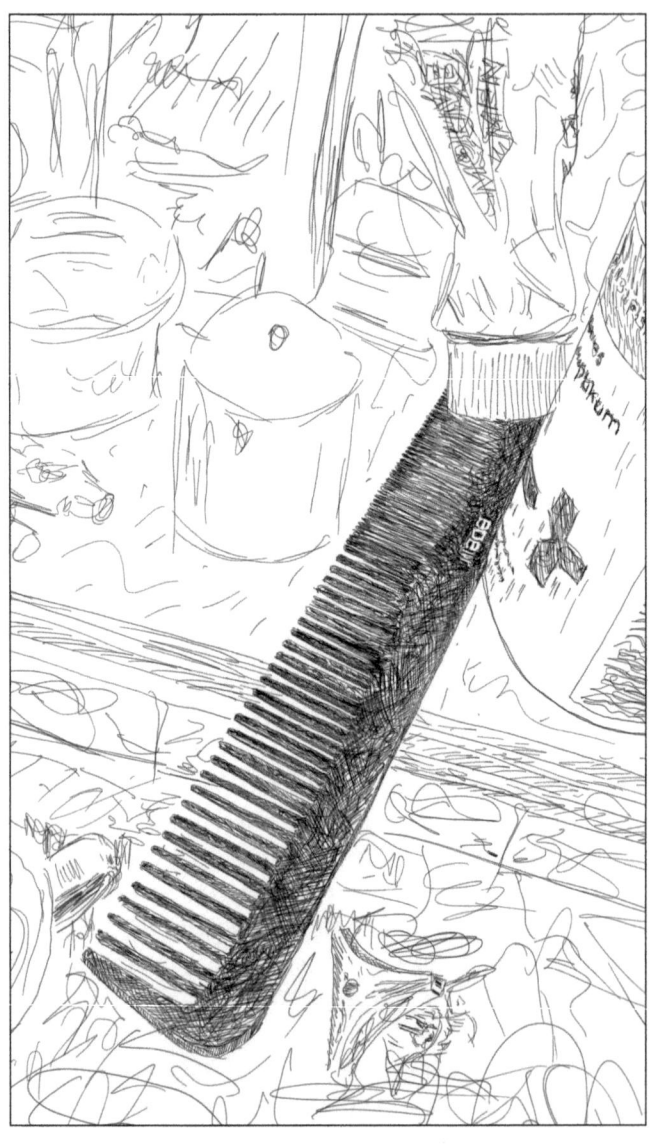

First the comb through the hair, then the jacket. Otherwise you could see the dandruff on the dark suit fabric. He would have to change the shampoo. The last recommendation of the shopping algorithm had only caused a terrible itching of the scalp. The dandruff thing was getting worse and worse

A critical look: Two visitors in person, sitting directly in front of him, that was something the CEO had to get used to again.

Polite

The two police inspectors were professionally business-like and almost restrainedly polite, not shirt-sleeved and leather-jacketed, as he had somehow unconsciously expected them to be. But then, this was reality and not an early evening series from the 1970s. The CEO's pulse went down again. He would probably not have to take the capsule with the blood pressure medication that he had already prepared. He briefly looked at the official order and had the commissioner in the system write a copy in the appropriate place in the directory tree. All according to regulations.

"You can look around here unhindered," the CEO said. He was now completely in business mode, "I'll show you anything you want to see."

It also worked in presence. It wasn't that much of a difference. He took a breath.

Of course, the commissioner could have asked where the CEO had been yesterday at 12. But that would have been ridiculous. You don't ask questions like that. That only happened in the old TV series.

"We'd like to ask you a few questions about your client, Tó Jan Mertens," said the younger of the two inspectors.

The CEO wiped through the interface of the management software.

"Yes, ... that was last week, right? You mean the contract termination on Tuesday?"

"Yes, Tuesday, late afternoon."

The CEO scrolled through the file. There was a will. The account manager had overlooked that. Right. But that wasn't really his job anymore, either. The customer had not given the company power of attorney beyond death. All the other messages had gone out correctly. Yes, the will could have been reported if the account manager had found something there. But all the data had been deleted by the customer. Only the contract data was still in the system. All data for which the customer was responsible had been completely deleted. Only the entry that the customer wanted it that way was still there.

The deletion process was designed in such a way that all media and constructions were disassembled into their basic components. Only the individual atoms remained. They then formed some kind of simple bonds. But that no longer had anything to do with the data they had once represented. The customer had set it up that way. This was not one of the standard processes. Some kind of security thing. There was nothing left that could be recovered from the deleted data.

The customer had been employed as a research scientist in a highly specialized scientific institute. They

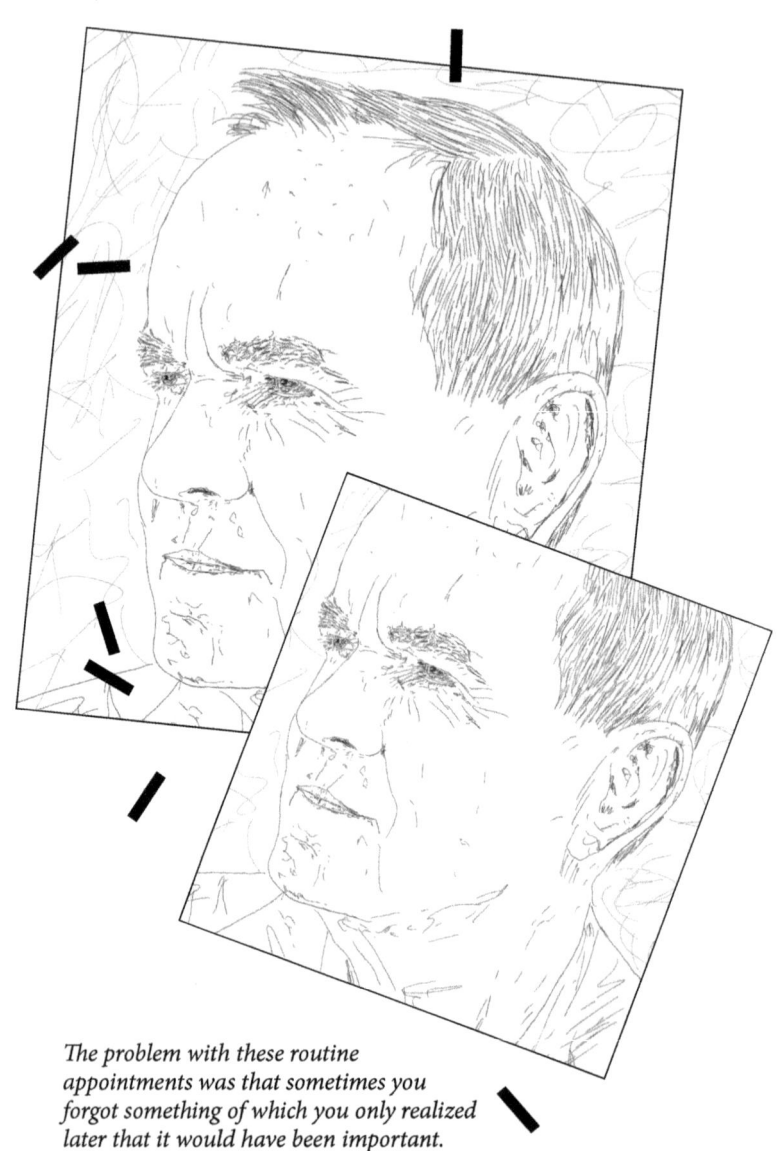

The problem with these routine
appointments was that sometimes you
forgot something of which you only realized
later that it would have been important.

60

needed such a high security level. It was all external technology. The customer had installed it himself. He had also registered it properly. Everything was documented. The customers had all the freedom they needed. They were a liberal management company. Only the rules of historic preservation had to be observed, of course, in the case of historic properties. But the protection of historical monuments had actually become more flexible.

The will was kept by a notary in Italy. An address in one of the smaller southern districts of Florence, Arceti. Why there of all places, the two commissioners could not say. But they had already checked the certificates. It was all correct. Only the fact that the contract termination had not been classified as reportable by the account manager had set them off.

Now the CEO was completely relaxed. This was just a routine visit. He was a business administrator. He sold the service provided by technology. He could calculate the costs. He didn't understand how the technology worked. Today, everyone assumed that technology was reliable. That was common sense. If something went wrong, that was a matter for the lawyers to sort out with the manufacturers. That's why he had the contract with the law firm. The agile ladies and gentlemen were expensive enough. He had done everything right.

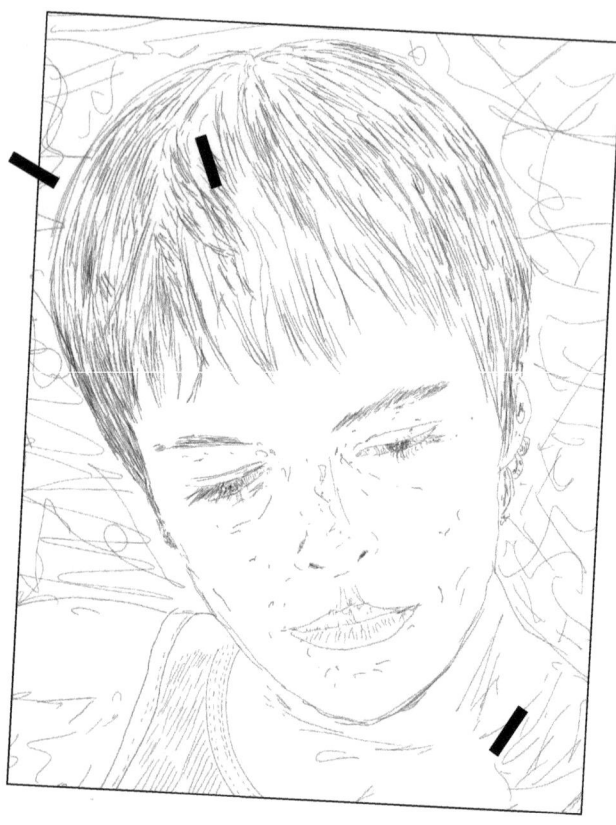

Paola thought the internship at the criminal investigation department was great. Of course, there was also a lot of routine work. But yesterday, for example, she had to work on a protocol that said something about a will at a notary in Arcetri. Today, that was a district of Florence. But in Arcetri there was still the Villa il Gioiello. Galileo Galilei, the man who discovered the moons of Jupiter, had spent the last years of his life there. And Jupiter was also the subject of the will. The commissioners had not seen this connection at all. Crazy.

Details

The inspectors asked for the entries from 2 p.m. to be viewed again.

The CEO clicked on the detailed view. It now showed every step.

The local service robot called the cleaner. The company had the R7 in use there. These were somewhat older but very robust systems, equipped with two AI modules. They ran independently of each other. Even in the event of a power failure, the machine could still make decisions autonomously and document them, even in a court of law. That was important.

The R7 immediately informed the mortician, as well as the local police, who then also came with the forensics team. All that was in the file of the system. He let the commissioners make a copy. Then they could check it again against the entries in their system. He would also copy the checksums. It would be possible to find out where the error had occurred that had brought them on the scene.

It was probably a simple transmission error. Perhaps it was also due to the many modified systems that the customer had installed. After all, this was unusual technology for a residential building. But the man had

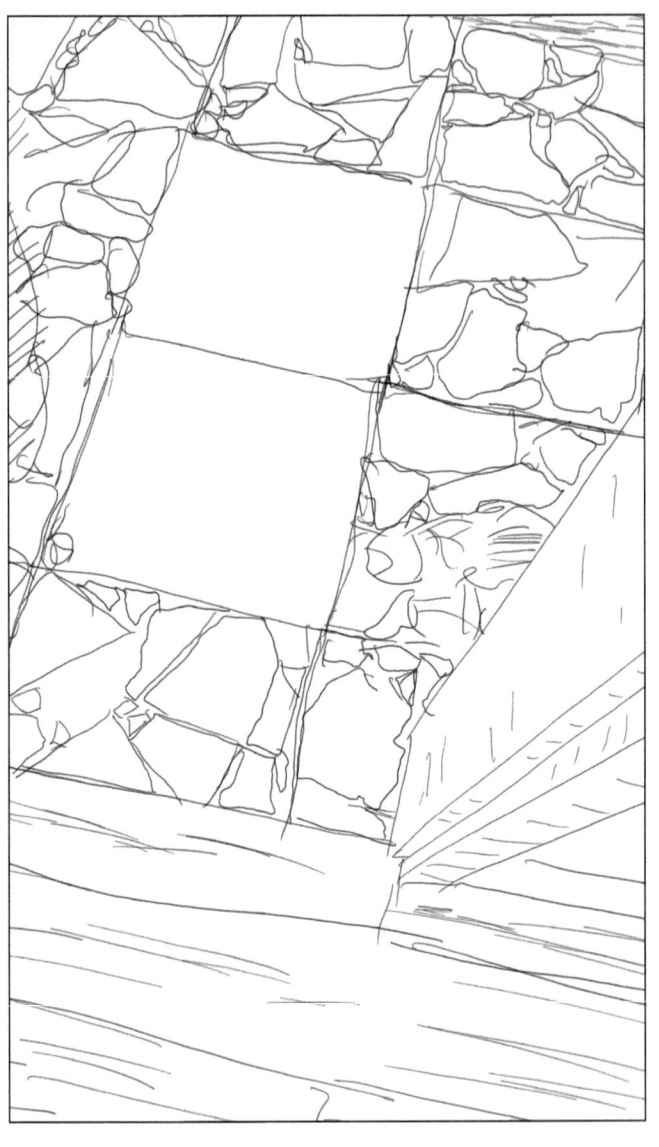

been a tech freak, a specialist. So unusual, yes, but inexplicable, no.

Of course, it was unusual for someone to delete all the data, completely and irrevocably, and to do so via an interface that was actually only supposed to control lighting and ventilation. But, as mentioned before, the customer was a tech freak. And it was okay for such specialists to play around with the home electronics. These guys did things with the home systems that the systems weren't actually intended for. That's where innovations came from. The CEO had a colleague whose son could control the mainframe computer in his father's startup via the game console display. He was six or so. So that wasn't normal, but it wasn't unusual either.

The commissioners asked about the possibility of electronics failure. That was another critical point. Missing safety interrogations, gesture control in places where haptic interaction was mandatory, and so on.

But that could be ruled out. These were all dual redundant Class One devices. They were full-featured. They were also certified for use in government buildings. Switched-off sensors or looped-through access points, that didn't exist there. The system never misunderstood an input. That was certain.

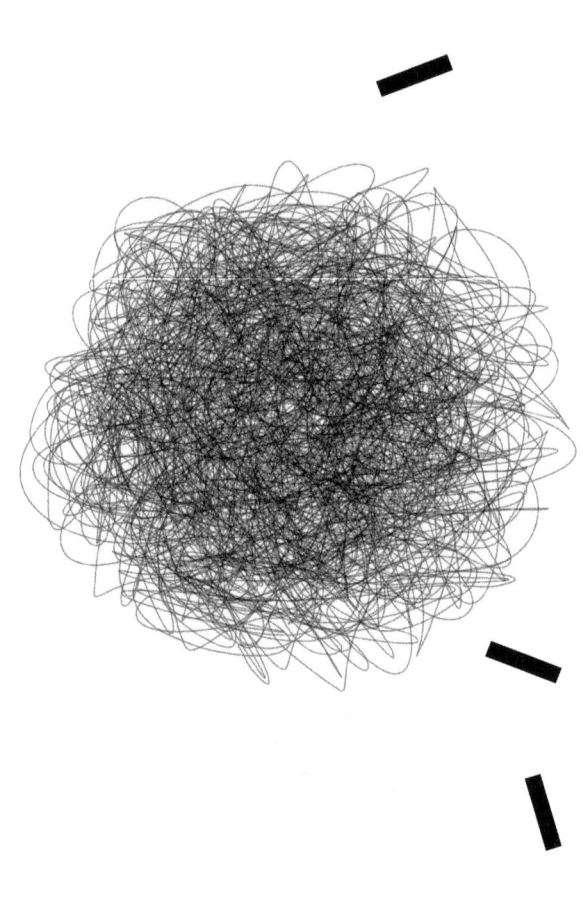

Wish

In the testament there was a passage which said something about the wish to be buried on Jupiter. The entire carbon was secured. The data in the protocols of the first cleaning robot and also those of the basic cleaner agree there. The estimate of the local robot was 23.8 kg. The then called R7 recorded 23.94 kg and the mortician was given 23.89 kg after certified measurement. This was all within the measurement tolerance. If one calculated that back, then that was so about 85 kg body weight. With 1,83 m of size that fit. The health data could be compared again, yes. But since the customer had deleted everything, locally, one would have to find out first who the family doctor was and so on. There now had been no central access to that data for several years. The customer probably also had private insurance. That was another system. In the central state system, at least, everything was signed out. There was only

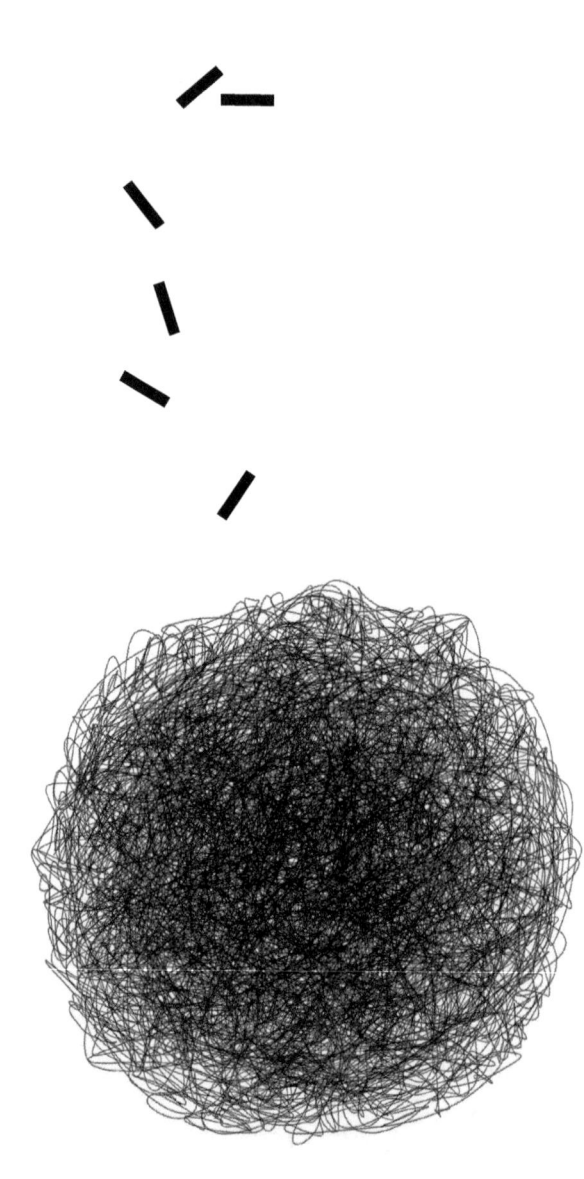

the entry about the record creation at birth. The deletion was really very complete. There were also people who didn't think it was right that, after the second major data protection reform, every citizen now had such far-reaching rights to dispose of his or her data.

Jupiter

The mortician was first and foremost a businessman. Nevertheless, the job meant that he could also have sentimental moments. There was nothing wrong with that. You just had to be careful that they didn't interfere with business.

He looked through the documents again. Sending an urn to Jupiter was something he had never done before. That was already extremely unusual. The usual orbits were actually the two near-Earth orbits, my1 and home2. These were meanwhile very well occupied. Already for some time only miniaturized urns, not larger than four centimeters, were allowed to be set out there. At the classical cremation, there was not much left. If you only regardet the weight portions, a dead body consisted, of 60 per cent oxygen, 30 per cent carbon and 10 per cent hydrogen, so Pi times thumb. Most of that went up the chimney as water vapor and CO_2. A system that actually extracted all the carbon from a human body was unusual. Morticians didn't work with such systems. They were much too expensive. This was already the mandate of a very exclusive customer.

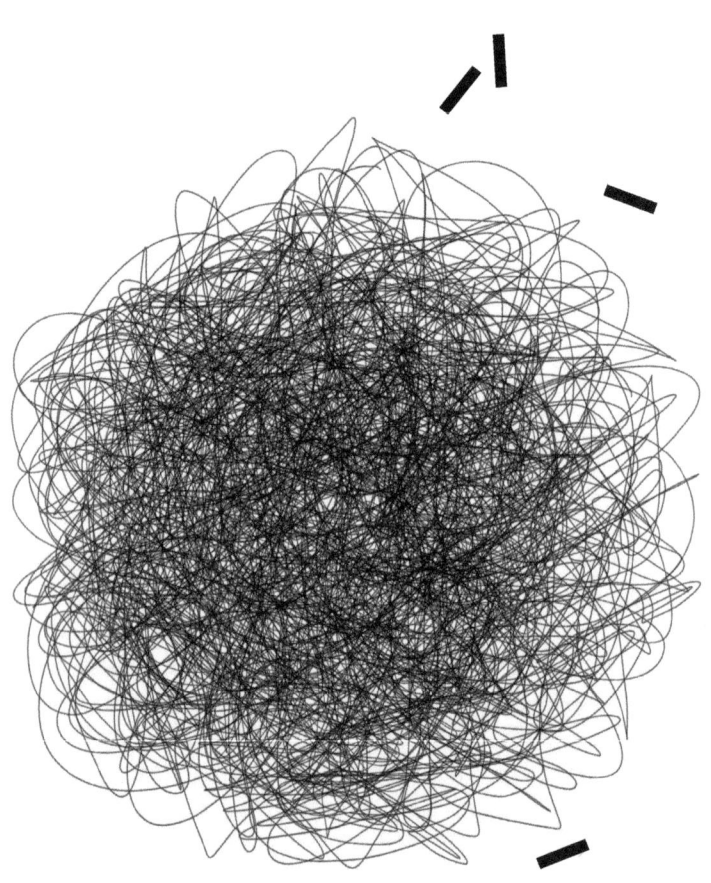

He would have documented the nearly two-year flight completely and in high resolution, including the drop of the urn from orbit onto the planet. These would be spectacular pictures, good publicity for him, and the customer had his will. It was, after all, the last one.

The mortician looked thoughtfully at the printed copy of the will. 23.89 kg of carbon on Jupiter. What would happen with it there?

Contents

Idea

Aftermath

About the authors

Alexandra Kirschbaum was born in Cologne in 1971. She studied musicology and Romance studies in Cologne and Hamburg. She wrote her dissertation on "The Italian in the Music of German Romanticism." For many years she has worked as a freelance editor and writes short stories and essays. Edition HIC< has published her two short stories "Tony" and "Die Freundin" and, as a separate volume, the novella "Augentropgen". Alexandra Kirschbaum is married to an architect and has two children.

Marcellus M. Menke is committed to the development and realization of projects in the fields of art, music, literature and education. In doing so, it is important to him to point out relationships and to make connections visible. In the editionHIC<, which he initiated and supervises, he publishes his own texts as well as texts by other authors that are important to him. Projects from the field of visual arts that he promotes find their home in the conTEMPart edition. In his project "buchmanufaktur.m4art.de" he creates books that will exist in the future. Together with the artist Michael A. Holst, he held an online creative workshop in the summer of 2020. In this process, he discovered his interest in drawing with the help of tablet computers. The illustrations created for this volume were based on ideas by Michael A. Holst and Paul Julius Kleiber.

Alexandra Kirschbaum
Augentropgen
Eine Zukunfts-Geschichte mit Illustrationen von Marcellus M. Menke

Edition HIC<

Ganz klein sind sie, die Viren, die schlagartig das Leben der menschlichen Gesellschaft verändert haben. Die Computer sind nicht davon betroffen. Sie organisieren das Leben der Menschen neu. Sicherheit hat oberste Priorität, denn Menschen sind wichtig, sagt das System. Menschen müssen geschützt werden.

Eine Zukunftsgeschichte, erzählt aus der Perspektive der Mitglieder einer durch und durch gewöhnlichen Familie in einer ganz und gar außergewöhnlichen Zeit. Eine beklemmende Zukunft, die heute näher nicht sein könnte. Irrationale Furcht und reale Gefahren bestimmen ein Leben zwischen wissenschaftlich-technischem Machbarkeitsglauben, erfahrener Ohnmacht und der Suche nach Auswegen aus einem hermetischen System, das eigentlich einmal geschaffen wurde, um ein besseres Leben zu ermöglichen.

Edition HIC< 2021 | ISBN: 9783753407647

Marcellus M. Menke

Wie Musik für die Augen zum Lesen

Geschenkte Gedichte
Köln 2015
ISBN: 9783837021738

Marcellus M. Menke

Für einige Augenblicke

Gedichte
Köln 2016
ISBN: 9783741256493

Marcellus M. Menke

Von innen heraus

Gedichte
Köln 2017
ISBN: 9783744852227

Marcellus M. Menke

Im Zeitstrom

Gedichte
Köln 2018
ISBN: 9783748171058

Marcellus M. Menke

Liebkosung

Wie eine zugeflogene Melodie
Gedichte
Köln 2019
ISBN: 9783750416246

Marcellus M. Menke

Konstruktion

Gedichte
2. Auflage, Köln 2022
ISBN: 9783756895687

Marcellus M. Menke

The English Poems of an Unknown German Poet

Poems
Cologne 2022
ISBN: 9783756223251

GESAMTAUSGABE

Marcellus M. Menke

Gedichte

Gesamtausgabe Band 1
1992 bis 2017
2. Auflage Köln 2020
ISBN: 9783750471214

Marcellus M. Menke

Gedichte

Gesamtausgabe Band 2
2018 bis 2019
Köln 2020
ISBN: 9783750471337

Marcellus M. Menke

Gedichte

Registerband
für Band 1 und 2 der
Gesamtausgabe
Köln 2020
ISBN: 9783750471344

editionHIC<

Marcellus M. Menke

Im hinteren Teil
des Himmels
ausgewählte Gedichte aus 27 Jahren
Köln 2020, ISBN: 9783752896855

Marcellus M. Menke

Zwischenbuch
Gedichte, Grafiken und Buchtitel
Durchgesehen und neu zusammengestellt auf der
Basis der Erstausgabe von 2005
Köln 2017, ISBN: 9783744812580

Le Tschen

Wie man die
Radioaktivität
überlebt
Siebenunddreißig mikroskopische
Erzählungen in drei Büchern
Aus dem Japanischen von Masahiro Miyamoto
Mit Nachworten von Marcellus M. Menke
Köln 2015, ISBN: 9783734791277

Marcellus M. Menke (Hrsg.)

Zukunftsgeschichten
Texte von Michael Quant,
Alexandra Kirschbaum, Brian T. Ballmoor
und Pascal-David Dombeaux
Köln 2017, ISBN: 9783743159266

editionHIC<

editionHIC<